# ALICE SCHERTLE

# MAISIE

## LYDIA DABCOVICH

LOTHROP, LEE & SHEPARD BOOKS    NEW YORK

*To my mother,*
*her children,*
*her grandchildren*
*and her great-grandchildren*

Text copyright © 1995 by Alice Schertle
Illustrations copyright © 1995 by Lydia Dabcovich
All rights reserved. No part of this book may be reproduced or utilized in any form or by any
means, electronic or mechanical, including photocopying and recording, or by any information
storage and retrieval system, without permission in writing from the Publisher. Inquiries should
be addressed to Lothrop, Lee & Shepard Books, a division of William Morrow & Company,
Inc., 1350 Avenue of the Americas, New York, New York 10019.
Printed in Hong Kong

First Edition    1   2   3   4   5   6   7   8   9   10

Library of Congress Cataloging in Publication Data
Schertle, Alice. Maisie / by Alice Schertle; illustrated by Lydia Dabcovich.
p.      cm. Summary: Follows the life of Maisie from her birth on a farm to her ninetieth
birthday party celebrated in a park with her large family.    ISBN 0-688-09310-8.—
ISBN 0-688-09311-6 (lib. bdg.)   I. Dabcovich, Lydia, ill.   II. Title.   PZ7.S3442Mai  1993
[E]—dc20   91-27549   CIP   AC

Maisie was born in a little red house in the shadow of a big red barn. Her first bed was a drawer Papa pulled right out of a dresser and set on the kitchen table, close to Mama.

Outside, chickens squawked, crows scolded, and a noisy stream tumbled through a meadow. The new baby heard it all, whenever she stopped crying long enough to listen.

When she was older, Maisie slept in the attic, in a real bed next to a little round window. At night she lay right under the roof, listening to owls. Sometimes she opened the window and answered them. "Who-WHOOO!"

In the daytime she played in the meadow, chasing chickens and running from the loud gray goose who chased her back.

She played in the big red barn, riding a dusty saddle on a wooden horse and, every now and then, finding something unexpected in the hay.

But most of all she played by the banks of the noisy stream, catching crawdads and, sometimes, jumping in, *Kerplunk!*

Then she shared her lunch with blue jays and ants, while bumblebees rumbled in the wildflowers and the hot sun dried her clothes.

At school Maisie did *eevy, ivy, OVERS* one hundred twenty-four times without a miss.

She could add a column of numbers faster than anyone except Lillian Templeton.

When Willard Parker pulled her braids, she punched him in the nose, so they both had to stay after school and write sentences.

She traded a brand new pencil for Eddie Bloom's frog, just so she could let it go. "Hop away home," said Maisie.

One day Walter Triggs brought Maisie a bouquet of bluebells and wild mustard. Maisie sniffed the flowers and sneezed. They both laughed.

Every day they drove to school together in Walter's rattle-trap car, Old Terrible.

On Saturdays they took long walks across the meadow, looking for beehives and owls' nests. Once they *forgot* to look for a bull in a pasture and had to run for their lives.

On soft summer evenings they went boating on a neighbor's pond. Sometimes Maisie rowed and Walter played the banjo.

In the autumn they both got after-school jobs sorting apples at a packing house.

On cold winter nights they ate popcorn and studied together by the fire.

At graduation, Maisie and Walter and the whole senior class had their picture taken. As soon as the camera clicked, they all threw their caps into the air.

One day Maisie and Walter were married. They packed Old Terrible with suitcases, boxes, and bags and moved away to the city. Old Terrible wheezed and popped and banged all along the way. When they got stuck in the mud a farmer hitched up his horse and pulled them out. Maisie gave the horse a cookie.

They moved into a little white house, just built.

"Such a quiet little house," said Maisie.

She planted flowers in back to bring the bees.

She planted a sycamore tree in front to bring the birds.

After a while there were bees and birds, and four children, too. Nothing was quiet anymore.

Maisie planted and weeded and watered her garden while her children ran and hollered and tumbled on the lawn. Sometimes, on hot summer days, she watered her children.

Dan fell off his bike and broke his leg. While he lay on the sofa with his leg in a cast, Walter taught him to play the banjo. Maisie brought him something unexpected to keep him company.

She helped Laura be a tree in the Christmas play. "If you're going to be a tree, be a good one," said Maisie. Everyone said Laura was the best tree they ever saw. When she came out on the stage, Walter stood right up and clapped.

Every spring Maisie and the children collected cocoons and watched butterflies unfold their paper-thin wings.

"Letting them go is the best part," Maisie told them.

"Fly away free," said Dan and Laura and Margaret and Charlie.

The flowers grew and the sycamore grew and the children grew and GREW and *GREW*, until they were taller than Maisie and it was time for them to go off and discover the world for themselves.

"Fly away free," said Maisie.

The children came home with books and pennants and T-shirts from college. Margaret brought a cowrie shell from the sea, Laura brought a tiny cactus from the bottom of a desert canyon, and once Charlie brought a pocketful of Mexican jumping beans. Dan brought a violin and played a sonata he had written himself.

Eventually they brought children of their own. Grandma Maisie tickled their tummies and told them tales and showed them bumblebees and bugs. Grandpa Walter drove them around in a big blue car that he called Terrible Too.

Every spring the grandchildren helped Maisie plant her garden. "Petunias and poppies for the bees, sunflowers for the birds, pumpkins for us," said Grandma Maisie.

They made a scarecrow and hung a basket of breadcrumbs on his arm. "So the birds will know he's friendly," said Elsie.

On warm summer days they walked to the park and helped Grandma Maisie feed popcorn to the pigeons.

On warm summer nights she took them out with a flashlight to watch crickets chirp.

In October they carved the pumpkins. Elsie and Mike drew the faces, Susan cut off the tops, and little Davey scooped out the insides with a spoon. "Save the seeds, Davey," said Grandma Maisie.

When winter snows piled up around the house, Walter and the grandchildren built Maisie a snowman. Maisie and Davey filled his hat with pumpkin seeds so the birds could help themselves.

One by one the grandchildren, too, went off to discover the world for themselves. They brought back photographs and friends from faraway places.

Mike came back in a pilot's uniform.

Elsie brought a telescope. Walter helped her set it up on the garage roof and Maisie took a look at the craters of the moon.

And once, when Davey roared up on a motorcycle, Grandma Maisie went for a ride.

Eventually the grandchildren came back with families of their own. Sometimes there were three or four great-grandchildren in the sycamore tree and one or two underneath it on Maisie's lap.

At night they all sat on the front porch, watching fireflies and learning from Maisie how to answer owls, "Who-WHOOO!"

On Maisie's ninetieth birthday, all the family—children, grandchildren, great-grandchildren, husbands, wives, aunts, uncles, and cousins—came together for a birthday picnic in the park. Walter played the banjo, Dan played the violin, and everyone sang, *"Happy birthday, dear Maisie…"*

Thirty-one great-grandchildren helped Maisie blow out the candles.

Fifteen pigeons helped clean up the crumbs.

After a while Maisie and her youngest great-granddaughter walked down to the banks of a noisy little stream that flowed through the park. Elizabeth stepped from rock to rock, looking for something in the water.

*Kerplunk!* Water splashed all over Maisie. Elizabeth held up a fat green frog.

"Isn't he beautiful!" said Maisie. "Feel how his heart ticks like a tiny clock."

Elizabeth put the frog gently down in the mud. "Letting them go is the best part," she said. "Hop away home."

Then Maisie and her youngest great-granddaughter walked back hand in hand, while bumblebees rumbled in the wildflowers and the summer sun dried their clothes.